I0519419

Wives Lend A

HOT EROTICA

Hand

by LEON RANDALL

WARNING

This book contains sexually explicit scenes and adult language. It may be considered offensive to some readers. This book is for sale to adults ONLY.

* * * * * * * * * * * * * * * * * * * *

Please store your files wisely where they cannot be accessed by underage readers.

Please feel free to send me an email. Just know that these emails are filtered by my publisher. Good news is always welcome.

Leon Randall - **leon_randall@awesomeauthors.org**

You might also want to check my blog for Updates and interesting info.
http://leon-randall.awesomeauthors.org/

Copyright © 2015 by Leon Randall

All Rights reserved under International and Pan-American Copyright Conventions. By payment of required fees you have been granted the non-exclusive, non-transferable right to access and read the text of this book. No part of this text may be reproduced, transmitted, downloaded, decompiled, reverse-engineered or stored in or introduced into any information storage and retrieval system, in any form or by any means, whether electronic or mechanical, now known, hereinafter invented, without express written permission of 4Fun Publishing. For more information contact 4Fun Publishing. The publisher does not have any control over and does not assume any responsibility for author or third-party websites or their content. This book is a work of fiction. The characters, incidents and dialogue are drawn from the author's imagination and are not to be construed as real. While reference might be made to actual historical events or existing locations, the names, characters, places and incidents are either products of the author's imagination or are used fictitiously, and any resemblance to actual persons living or dead, business establishments, events or locales is entirely coincidental.

About the Publisher

4Fun Publishing, a member of **BLVNP Incorporated,** 340 S. Lemon #6200, Walnut CA 91789, info@blvnp.com / legal@blvnp.com
NOTE: Due to the highly emotional reaction of some people to works of erotic fiction, any email sent to the above address that contains foul language or religious references is automatically deleted by our anti-spam software and will not be seen. All other communications are welcome.

DISCLAIMER

Please don't be stupid and kill yourself. This book is a work of FICTION. Do not try any new sexual practice that you find in this book. It is fiction and not to be confused with reality. Neither the author nor the publisher or its associates assume any responsibility for any loss, injury, death or legal consequences resulting from acting on the contents in this book. Every character in this book is over 18 years of age. The author's opinions are not to be construed as the opinions of the publisher. The material in this book is for entertainment purposes ONLY. Enjoy.

Wives Lend A Hand

Hot Erotica

By: Leon Randall

© **Leon Randall 2015**
ISBN: 978-1-68030-446-6

This was a unique occasion in my 56 year life. I was completely naked with a rampant hard-on in the company of my darling wife (who, of course, had seen my extended appendage a million times before) but also in the company of another couple, for whom seeing my erection was a first-time experience. As a group we were transitioning from being just friends to friends plus 'more'. Russell and I were sitting on the sofa in Jan's and my house, a couple of feet apart, each with our hands tucked at our sides so we couldn't touch our dicks. That was the deal we'd agreed to. We were being watched by our wives who were sitting on the ends of the sofa, enjoying our 'situation'. An hour before, this would have been embarrassingly unthinkable. But now, each of us had our Willies about as engorged and scarlet-purple as it's possible to be, both of us were hard and oozing precum and, at least in my case, throbbing and close to a hair trigger which any moment was threatening to see me tip over that edge and come messily all over myself, hands-free and without even being touched. Sound impossible? I would have thought so, too, until that Saturday afternoon.

* * *

We met Eva and Russell via a nudist website. If you've read some of our other stories you'll know how Jan and I fumbled our way into nudism. I won't go into all that again here, but the highly summarised version is that when our son moved out of the house to live-in at university we suddenly found ourselves able to be all frisky again in ways that you really can't be when your kids live at home. I'm pleased to say that Jan and I genuinely still love each other - are still 'in love' might be a nice way to put it - and are enjoying a revitalised sex life with this newly-found empty-nest freedom. To our mutual surprise and enjoyment we have learned a new thing or two about each other's sexual desires as a result (amazing that after years of marriage that can happen, but it can) and discovered we shared some interests in exhibitionism and voyeurism. We'd led an enjoyable but pretty tame sex life until recently so this opened up exciting possibilities - at least in theory. We were both timid about turning those thoughts into reality. We're both possessive of each other and didn't want new and naughty sexual 'fun' to turn out to be not fun at all and leave us jealous or unhappy that we'd gone too far, too fast. In that context, swinging has a tantalising appeal in theory but we agreed neither of us really wanted that so we looked for softer options. We put our toe in the nudism water as a fairly obvious early step. It promised to be a bit naughty but not likely to get us arrested or divorced. And by its nature (no pun intended) it promised to provide chances to see and be seen. We had aspirations for 'more' than just that, but wanted to take it slowly. So, that's how we met with Eva and Russell.

Of course, we stared with the Internet; where else? I did a bit of surfing and 'research' to get my head around the nudist and naturist scene, where the beaches are, and so on. I also found a nudist website which I joined and created a profile. This is one of those sites where it's a bit like a dating site, with discussion forums and so on, but where the core purpose of the site is to read other people's profiles and for them to read yours with the opportunity to then send messages to each other if you like what you read and want to meet up in person. There's some art, some science and a bit of black magic in creating the right profile that tells enough of the truth whilst throwing the right hints, and also sets the 'bar' at the right height for what timidity level you have. It's quite tricky to find the balance.

One of the things I quickly learned about nudists is that there are serious ones and not-so-serious ones. The serious ones are genuine in their commitment to 'the lifestyle' and would spend most waking moments without clothes if they could. They have disdain for those not-so-serious types who would sully the purity of true nudism with any form of eroticism. For the purists (I might almost say Puritans) these things are like oil and water: they just don't mix. As for the second group of the not-so-serious, there are many shades of grey, and therein lies both opportunity and trouble if you misread someone's shade. So, back to creating a profile: what does one say if, like us, you are ready to try nudism because it seems a bit naughty, seems like it might be fun, holds the promise of seeing some nice exposed body parts you wouldn't normally see, presents the chance to try out a bit of flaunting of the attributes you have, and also holds the tantalising prospect of 'more' if you want it? If you read profiles on a nudist site you'll quickly get the drift of the groups I have described and how tricky this is. If, in the end, you are wanting to hook-up with people who are likely to fit with your desires without you disappointing them for one reason or another, and them not disappointing or intimidating you, it's not easy. But, despite it being quite a task, we did it, as you will read. Our profile was truthful about our age and newness in trying out the nudist scene, said we were not looking for swingers but that we thought of ourselves as open minded.

It was pleasantly surprising that we received quite a number of contacts, most of whom had profiles that we thought were 'ok' (and some who didn't and who obviously couldn't read). Amongst the nicer ones was that of Russell and Eva. They were a couple about our age, with kids off their hands (except for weekend visits home to do the washing). Their profile said they were mostly interested in nudism at home around the pool and were looking for nudist-oriented new friends to share "a bit of a laugh". Now, I don't want to dwell on this, but I should explain that that phrase is used a lot in the nudist context. Whilst at the time I didn't know, now I believe it usually means "we're open to being playful in the right circumstances".

We exchanged some emails then had a chat on the phone, ultimately agreeing to meet for lunch at a nice pub we both knew. It's a bit strange - at least we found it so - getting to the point of setting up a meeting like this. It's a complex mixture of overt factors and some covert ones. Obviously you need to feel some potential for a friendly connection on a purely social level and be convinced enough that the profile you read translates more or less to truth. I'm sorry if this sounds discriminatory, but in that situation you don't want to be surprised that the people have misrepresented themselves or have characteristics that make you feel uncomfortable. Of course, they are feeling exactly the same sense of uncertainty. That's all pretty true of any social quasi-blind-date situation, but overlay on that a more subtle agenda. To start with, the common factor to the planned meeting is nudism which, most would agree, is not mainstream behavior for most people. Then overlay on that an added complexity of discerning what type of nudism, purist or not, that these potential friends enjoy and want to find in other likeminded souls. Then, on top of all that, there's the 'more' agenda. Does 'a bit of a laugh' mean they want humorous new friends, or is it code for friends with benefits? When they read 'open minded' are they thinking we're some kind of intense philosophers of the Kant school, or that we have a sexy agenda of 'more' in the back of our minds? See? I told you it wasn't easy.

Lunch turned out to be great. On the social level they were nice, friendly, articulate, civilised people, it was easy to like them. On the physical level which, yes, does play a part in these things, they were each carrying a few more pounds than Jan or I did, but were still a handsome couple. To put it bluntly, the idea of seeing them nude was not suddenly derailed by the reality of having met them in person. They must have felt much the same about us because from that lunch 'date' (and it was sort of a 'date') we agreed to meet again, next time at their house.

Odd though it may seem, whilst we obviously chatted during lunch about nudism and our experiences with it so far (some beach visits in our case, mainly home nudism for them, plus a swim night as visitors at a nudist club, which they said they didn't enjoy much), there was no explicit agreement or 'agenda' that our next social encounter would be nude. That was just left unstated, perhaps presumed. I should also explain here that the 'more' part of our fledgling and hopefully growing friendship simply was not part of the discussion that first day. There were moments in the flow of conversation where a remark or a joke was (perhaps) a disguised hint, but nothing overt. I know Jan and I had presumably typical hang-ups over the years and took a long time to bravely branch out in our sex life, but it can't just be us who feels that timidity. Eva and Russell either felt it too and therefore didn't feel comfortable putting it 'out there' that they wanted friends with 'more' or, perhaps, they really didn't want that at all and 'a bit of a laugh' for them meant just that. Again I say, see what I mean about it being tricky?

Our next meeting at their place was again to be a lunch, a BBQ around their pool. By luck it was a beautiful day so swimming was likely to be realistic (as opposed to being determined to get in but shivering while doing so). Of course, we were entirely clothed as we arrived (who drives nude?) and our hosts were too as they greeted and welcomed us into their home. We were impressed as they showed us through to the outdoor patio and pool area and its relaxed-style set-up, just right for entertaining. We exchanged the "how are you?" greetings and were fussed over as they arranged drinks, then we settled in around the table and, oddly and awkwardly, the time to 'get nude' had sort-of passed. See how inexperienced we all were? With hindsight, an invitation to 'get changed' or some other euphemism would have had the clothes off earlier than we eventually managed. Not that we were stressing about it, but we had presumed that today would be a sans clothes day; indeed, we wanted it to be, and as we all chatted it was taking quite a while for us to get around to that topic.

I am not normally socially adventurous but am pleased to say that, surprising myself and surprising Jan hugely (as well as our hosts!) I bravely led the way. I decided that this was one of those times in life to 'just do it'. Asking directions to the bathroom, I went upstairs, ostensibly for a pee, and took my gear off, then reappeared on the patio entirely naked with Mr Happy hanging right out there (limply of course). It caused a notable pause in the conversation, that's for sure! I filled the moment's silence with some banality along the lines of, "Well, it's a good-to-be-nude day for me. I hope you'll join me." There was an excruciating one or two seconds when noone spoke, during which I felt completely uncomfortable and out of place. "What about you, Darling?" I said in Jan's direction and, I'm annoyed to remember, she actually looked uncertain as if it was OK to leave me 'out there' as the only nude person on this very-clothed patio. Then, bless her, the moment of uncertainty was replaced with what I presume was a "Why not?" decision as she responded with, "Good idea. Lovely day for it. What about you guys.....?" You could almost see the 'dot, dot, dot, question-mark' dangling in the air. It was Eva who said, "Sorry. I don't know why we didn't lead the way. Just a bit shy I suppose," and the matter had been resolved.

Jan went off the bathroom I had used, as our hosts went to their bedroom. Minutes later Jan was back with me and moments after that Eva and Russell appeared again, this time in the flesh, as it were. I think we all felt a tiny bit embarrassed with everybody speaking pretty much at the same time to the effect of, "Welcome back. Isn't this much better?" The embarrassed moment passed in a flash.

It's funny, looking back, or perhaps I am reading too much into it, but I had the sense that we were all trying to pretend this was entirely normal for us (which it wasn't) and that we weren't interested in having a look at our now-nude companions (which we were). I've told you about Jan in other stories so I'll be brief here and say she's a pretty, curly-haired blonde with a full-but-not-fat figure, still-yummy breasts, a lovely firm bottom and a hairless pussy. All in all, good enough to eat (but I digress....). Eva and Russell were a fine nude couple with no great surprises; after all, in the end, what surprises can there be? We know there'll be bums and nipples and dicks, and indeed there they all are! It's funny how un-sexy it all is when you actually do this, but you can't help yourself looking, anyway. Eva, as I said, is a little larger than Jan but attractive and well-proportioned. Her tummy, being bigger and a bit droopy, made it hard to see her pussy at-a-glance, but her breasts were sizable and shapely with large nipples on full, prominent view. Predictably, I had less interest in Russell but took in his salient features just the same. He, too, had a few extra pounds he could afford to lose; the sort of body that would be called 'portly' but not fat. His rounded tummy was his most notable feature which, coupled with his slightly balding head, was suggestive of what a caricaturist would make the most of if drawing him. Interesting for me, and Jan as I later found when discussing the day, was that Russell had a very withdrawn penis. Never having been especially sporty, I haven't routinely been in male change-room situations where other men's attributes are on clear show. Perhaps because of that absence of life experience I found Russell's almost-invisible penis a surprise. I know all guys have a small dick at times, but flaccid usually means dangly-but-measurable. In Russell's case, it was withdrawn to the point of not being 'dangly' at all; just a little pink head peeking from its hidey-hole location atop his balls and surrounded by fuzzy, slightly red-coloured, pubic hair. Oh well: apparently we're all different despite being all the same.

The afternoon passed delightfully. Good food, good wine, pleasant company, lovely weather and a pool to dip into. Again, perhaps oddly, or perhaps this is what the 'serious nudists' mean, despite the fact that we were sitting there naked, there was nothing notably sexy or even suggestive about that state of undress once you get beyond the fact that it's happening at all. Once you've seen the nudity, looked at the nipples and so on, they don't suddenly look different when looking again. So, it was mostly like any other pleasant social afternoon amongst people who are already superficially friendly and are getting to know one another better. I need to add that there was no time when the conversation overtly turned to 'more'. This was entirely fine by us; it wasn't the key agenda item that was to make or break a successful day or, for that matter, a successful relationship with these nice people. But the back of my mind was attuned to noticing any hints that may be thrown out there along those lines, and there were a couple where I pricked up my ears.

It seems silly now that, as I'll explain, we've moved far beyond that timidity with our new friends but at the time noone was quite sure. It turns out both couples wanted 'more' but neither knew quite how to say it. It's quite a complex social 'dance' with neither couple being of a social style to use or want to hear overtly sexual innuendo and smut, so anything that was going to emerge at the fledgling time in the relationship was going to be subtle and have the opportunity to back-track if it caused offence. Likewise, picking up and responding to a hint or opportunity to take the conversation along the lines of 'more' brought with it the possibility of misreading what had been said and embarrassing everyone in so doing. Pathetic, isn't it? But these are the real-life tribulations of couples feeling their way and taking it slowly.

During the course of our chatter which ranged across many topics, we naturally talked a little about nudism, why we had each found that worth a try, what each couple had done with it, and the like. Our hosts said that Russell in particular had liked the idea of being an at-home nudist for a long time but it was awkward to indulge until their kids had left home. Eva went along with it but said she was a bit less enthusiastic - more because she felt the cold, she said, than for prudish or other reasons. It seems they both enjoyed their pool in the nude on many a night as well as during the day as we will be doing that afternoon, well shielded, I should add, from neighbors' eyes by dense foliage. In the course of their remarks I'm pretty sure I picked up a meaningful smirk as they shared a recollection of those nights in the pool. They mentioned again the swim night they had visited at a nearby nudist club but said they'd found it quite unwelcoming.   And then Eva surprised us by dropping into the chatter that she and Russell had visited a Couples Club a while back. Wow! This was more than Jan and I had ever dared to contemplate and was undoubtedly in the realm of 'more', yet Eva delivered that gem in such a matter-of-fact way that it didn't invite salacious questions. She said they hadn't been especially impressed, and felt themselves a bit too old for it, and left it at that.

Hmmmm. Interesting. Jan and I discussed it later. That they'd done it at all invited a much wider speculation about our new friends' horizons than we had 'officially' discovered. Couples clubs are places for swinging, partner swapping, group gropes and group sex, fucking for an audience and much more - all of which sounds titillating but has not been on Jan's and my agenda. Having met and coming to know Russell and Eva, I couldn't quite picture them in that scene but, hey! Good on them for bravely giving it a try - and, a little curiously, mentioning it 'in passing', or so it seemed. As I say, Hmmmm.

As the afternoon drew to a close, we all re-clothed ourselves and said our farewells with plans to email each other for a follow-on social engagement - which turned out to be the afternoon of the day I mentioned at the beginning, with Russell and me 'at full salute' under the watchful (and, I think, admiring) gaze of our wives. That came about because of a chain of events related to a thing called "Sexpo" which was the catalyst for our next social encounter.

If you don't have a Sexpo in your country or city, I should explain that it is basically a commercial exhibition based around adult toys - a sort of sex shop on steroids. It's a surprisingly large and well-attended annual event in our city which Jan and I visited last year for the first time.   Spread across a large pavilion in one of the city's main exhibition hubs, it presents the browsing adults-only visitor with all the latest in sex aids and toys, books and videos (all of which, of course, are for sale) as well as a number of other entertainments to amuse and titillate the patrons. There are strip shows, pole dancing and various stage acts, mostly involving little clothing. There was a guy who painted caricatures on canvass by dipping his penis in paint and using it as the 'brush' (true!) together with various opportunities for, and prizes for, brave visitors to get involved in some of the exhibits. An amusing example that kept and held quite a crowd of onlookers was where female visitors could ride the Sybian orgasmatron (in any state of undress they liked which, disappointingly but predictably, meant fully clothed when we were watching). Amazingly, some women actually did take up the offer, eliciting a spectrum of responses from the riders ranging across embarrassed laughter to "oh my God" genuine looks of surprise and intense enjoyment. None rode it to an orgasmic denouement, though. Pity. All in all, Sexpo is quite a fun event though in reality less sexy than it sounds.

Hearing this event was coming up in the calendar, and wanting to go again ourselves to see what was new in the realm of erotic tools and toys, it occurred to us to ask Eva and Russell if they'd like to come along to share the fun. A couple of emails later, it was agreed. It turned out they'd heard of and been intrigued about Sexpo before but had never been, so were quite open to the idea. It was agreed we'd meet at our house, share our car to the venue, enjoy the exhibition and come back to our place for afternoon refreshments.

As Jan and I thought about that forthcoming social encounter there were some new ingredients to consider. She and I continued to share the anticipation of 'more' in a relationship with new friends: that was one of the reasons for this whole journey. That aspect had been slow to develop with Eva and Russell so far but the pace had suited our timidity. Now, having come to know them well enough to feel that 'more' was an agreeable prospect, we were ready for that to develop, even to help the agenda along a little if the opportunity presented. However, we agreed to remain attuned to their reaction and if it looked like we had misread their mutual interest in 'more', we'd back off.

In that frame of mind, the anticipation of our next encounter with our new friends brought a frisson of excitement. Whereas the shared nudity with them had proved enjoyable, even fun, of itself it hadn't been sexy or erotic. But, this next social engagement had a new ingredient: it was unmistakable that Sexpo was about sex. Simply visiting the exhibition with another couple automatically meant, at the very least, that sex was on the conversation agenda and from that starting point interesting possibilities and lowered inhibitions were likely to emerge. We were open to those possibilities.

Our friends arrived at our place late morning as agreed and after exchanged kisses and handshakes in greeting we headed off to the city in our car. During that twenty minute drive and encouraged by the context we exchanged chatter about the idea of Sexpo, and about sex shops in general. We thereby discovered from each other that both couples enjoyed the occasional visit to one. We told them a funny story about the day we bought some naughty videos at our favourite sex shop and then left them by accident at the restaurant where we had lunch following our shopping expedition, and the embarrassment I felt in going back later to collect them! As we lined up for our tickets and then proceeded to the venue entry Eva was comfortably chatting about how she and Russell use an online sex-shop occasionally for toys and videos. Hmmmm.

Stepping through the curtained entrance which prevented those outside from too many free glimpses we were confronted with a glittering and raucous pageant: row upon row of commercial booths, colourfully set-up with eye-catching signs, awash with sequins-and-tinsel décor that exhibited no taste at all, a-glow and a-flash with look-at-me lighting of every sort and pleasantly noisy with a mix of music and sound effects from every direction, plus the chatter of people. Lots of people. The place was simply buzzing.

We stood for a minute consulting the exhibit guide that was handed over as part of the entry process and agreed a general plan-of-attack that would guide us around all the larger exhibits and stage events. Although we also agreed where and when we'd meet up if we drifted in different directions, for the most part we strolled along as a foursome, taking it all in, exchanging some chatter along the way. Almost the first 'port of call' was a huge display of every sort of dildo you can imagine. Small and large, multi-colored and glow-in-the-dark, some that looked very hi-tech with beads that undulated around the outside and shaped pistons that went up and down, around and about. Fascinating. And these weren't all just in bubble packs you couldn't touch. Helpful (and shapely, scantily clad) models were handing passers-by working models to feel and look at close-up. I thought for a moment this was going to be a little awkward and embarrassing but that thought passed quickly as Eva weighed an elaborately-constructed, rocket-ship-shaped 'engine' in her hand that was writhing and pulsing as she held it, and commented, "Wow! I reckon I'd like to try one of *these*!" With that, any residual ice was broken and our joint conversations as we made our way through the exhibits was frank, at times quite raunchy and often funny as well.

"I should buy myself one of these," said Jan, pointing to a hard plastic erect dildo-dick which seemed about the size of a baseball club, complete with a shapely, realistically-colored knob and veins. "What for," I responded, "when you've got me?" "Oh, I'm bigger than that," Russell chimed in. "Twice as big," Eva added, "but only after the tablets".

We weren't always sweeping along as a tight group of four but instead loosely browsed, rummaged, fossicked and chortled our way along, admiring the exhibits and some of the exhibitors, pausing now and then to see a few minutes of the little stage shows here and there. Along the way we each made some purchases. We were with them when Eva did indeed buy an exotic-looking dildo: an aqua-coloured thing in a hard plastic bubble pack that looked like it needed a license to drive. They were with us when Jan and I bought one of those all-purpose has-a-bit-of-everything-you-need vibrator sex-aid kits and there was a bit of suggestive commentary about the anticipated enjoyment to be had from the anal beads that were included. We probably spent about 2 hours there altogether and as we headed for the exit there were a few bags of purchases between us.

Chatter on the way home was about the exhibits and some of the side-show-style entertainments: notably the dick-using cartoonist mentioned before, the pole dancing (and the humorous suggestion that Russell should have had a go), the orgasmatron and some interesting speculation about whether those electric stimulator gadgets actually do encourage women to orgasm. All in all, it was a highly entertaining and definitely not prudish discussion we were having, and were still having as we arrived at our place, parked the car and moved ourselves into the house, dragging our collective purchases along.

Again, it had probably been assumed rather than explicitly said between us that this was to be a nude social occasion. It certainly was a beautiful day, our patio area is secluded when we want it to be behind louvers, and so it was quickly agreed that we'd 'nude up' as the saying goes amongst those who do it. We rustled-up towels, pointed out the bathroom and showed our guests to a spare bedroom to de-clothe themselves. Russell made some remark that if they weren't down in 15 minutes we should come and find them, and patted Eva on the bottom as he said it. She giggled and joined in the joke, adding if that happened we might as well join them. Mere banter, but suggestive just the same. It was clear that the mood of our relationship with these nice people was moving into the land of 'more'.

Jan and I exchanged glances as we left our friends to change and remarked to each other as we took our gear off in our own room that the afternoon was possibly heading towards frisky. We agreed we were each fine with that and to see where things went without getting too carried away.

A few minutes later it turned out that we didn't need to go find the others; they found their way down the stairs to meet us on the patio where drinks and snacks were ready. With the customary spreading of towels on the outdoor furniture, the now-nude four of us settled in to continue our chat. Again I admired Eva's quite pronounced nipples and I could see Russell trying to be subtle about checking out Jan's charms, upper and lower.

We hadn't really eaten a proper lunch because of the timing of our exhibition visit so, it being late afternoon by this stage, we agreed that an early dinner was a good idea. I'm the main cook in our house so it fell to me to organise the meats and salads for dinner as the others continued their chatter and sipped their drinks. As I buzzed in and out from the kitchen I could follow much of the conversation, which continued to more or less focus on the day's event, with sex and eroticism pretty much always near the surface of the chatter. As the main part of the meal was done and we began grazing on cheese and crackers, Jan had the bright idea of asking, "So, what else did you guys buy?"

"You mean, apart from what will become my new, battery-powered best friend?" Eva responded. "We'd probably be too shy to say," she said, pausing. "Unless you show us what you bought, too," she finished with a grin. "What do you say, baby? Shall we reveal our bad taste and disgraceful tendencies to these nice people?"

"They'll never look at us the same way again," Russell said in response, sipping his wine. "But, then again, maybe they're more disgraceful than we are, in which case we'll own the moral high ground." To this, Jan added, "Low though it may turn out to be," and we all laughed.

There followed some fossicking around inside the house to retrieve the various bags that had transported assorted 'disgraceful items' home and a couple of minutes later we were settled back outside in the late afternoon balmy air, still quite naked and passing around the table the various things we'd bought amidst much guffawing and good natured ribald commentary. Eva's battery-powered dildo looked like something NASA might send to Mars. Its instruction book, which was an amazing ten pages or so, had us hooting with laughter as its Asiatic 'English' gave advice about insertion, speed control and a health warning to avoid over stimulating of female parts in case of fainting. Jan and I had bought that multi-purpose all-in-one sex aid kit and as that was passed around the discussion speculated on various uses of its assorted bits and pieces. The penile sleeve stimulator attachment drew a remark from Russell who said it looked very promising, the beads again merited a mention with Eva saying frankly that she and Russell enjoyed those and wondering out loud what culture had invented them. Jan's tiny battery-powered nipple clamps came out next. "Now you know what turns me on," she said to the four winds, to which Eva added, "Ooooh, don't they look good?" and reached to take one for a closer inspection. Each clamp had a little button cell battery already installed and in a moment Jan had one of the gadgets buzzing excitedly in her hand. "Goodness, it's an enthusiastic little devil," she said and, apparently without really thinking about it (so she told me later), touched the buzzing object to her left nipple. "My God," she gasped. "Two of these at once and a girl would pass out!" She added, looking playfully at me, "I know what I'll be doing later."

As the buzzy nipple toys went back into the bag, Jan turned to Russell who, until then, hadn't confessed to buying anything. "What about you, Mister? Jan asked. "How about you impress us with the bad taste of your purchases?"

"With the bar already set so low," Russell grinned, "my modest purchase almost raises the tone." He continued, "Indeed, nothing so tawdry as gadgets for me. My choice was purely cerebral," he intoned, putting on a school-masterly voice, as he produced a DVD from a bag. "Behold, a visual feast of, I am sure, high intellectual quality, which I am looking forward to in order to improve my mind." He waved the DVD around.

"What is it? Stop waving it and let's have a look," Jan interrupted, reaching out whilst Russell handed it over. "Oh yes, I see what you mean," she remarked, reading the title and glancing with artificial sternness at Russell and then at Eva and me . "Hand Job Heaven. I have no doubt it is very profound."

Russell looked a bit embarrassed so I felt some rescue remarks were called for. "You can't beat a good hand job, I always say. Better than sex. Isn't that right, Russell?"

Before he could answer, Eva put in, "It's one of his favourites, that's for sure," to which Jan added, "They're pretty popular in this house too, aren't they Honey?"

"Absolutely right," I responded. "All a result of your talent and dexterity, arts no doubt learned as part of a misguided but excellent Catholic girls-school education." Warming to the subject, I went on, "When you get going, I am mere putty in your hands. Well, hard putty," I finished lamely, but everybody chuckled.

Jan began reading from the back cover. "Over ninety minutes of throbbing, pulsing cum coaxed from hard cocks by skilled hands. More than 200 scenes of non-stop, cock-stroking action. Gallons of squirting jizz. Cum on. Join the fun". She stopped reading and looked enquiringly at Russell, her eyebrows raised. He just smiled back.

"As I say, an intellectual DVD," he responded, raising his own eyebrows.

"Well, it sounds like you'll enjoy it," Eva said, looking at Russell. "I might even enjoy it with you," she added with a grin, "though two hundred scenes might test my interest." "Who knows, darling," she went on, "I might learn some new tricks."

This whole repartee shared with our friends was fun and amusing, and it was definitely straying into more explicit sexually-oriented territory. Maybe Jan picked up that thought, too, because I heard her saying, "Why don't we have a peek now? We've finished eating, so let's improve our minds with the prospect of exciting new knowledge."

Although I am sure, and Jan confirmed later, that she hadn't contrived that suggestion to be a trigger point, it proved to be. If you can imagine the scene I have been describing, there's a distinct line between amusing sexually-oriented chatter and actually sharing with others the watching of sexually explicit video material. There was a momentary silence as Jan's question hung in the air. Eva spoke first, saying,

"Although my talents in this regard are exceptional, there's always room for improvement, I suppose."

Russell was smiling but looked a tiny bit uncomfortable. "Having bought the thing, I certainly plan on watching it, but to tell the truth, I might embarrass myself and you ladies if we watch it now." He went on, "You may have forgotten, but we don't have any clothes on and, purely because of the intellectual stimulation, you understand, well... " He paused. "Blood might divert from my brain to elsewhere, if you get my drift."

The same thought had gone through my mind. With women, arousal is more subtle and disguised, but men get hard-ons. Whilst getting a bit verbally frisky with our new friends was fun, and 'more' was possibly somewhere on our future agenda, watching skin flicks of any sort in nude company was asking for erections to pop up. This was definitely new territory in our relationship with our friends.

Jan moved the conversation ahead, picking up Eva's point as a humorous challenge. "I have it on reliable authority," she said, ostentatiously nodding in my direction, "that these," she wiggled her fingers, "are amongst my greatest assets. But, like you, Eva," she went on, "I am open to ongoing learning. I'll put the thing in and we'll see what we see."

With that, she bustled away from the table and started pressing buttons on our TV system. We three others continued to sit at the outdoor table for a couple of seconds, looking at each other, until we heard Jan call, "Come on in, folks. Some Academy Award performances await." Grabbing Jan's towel and my own, I headed indoors with our two friends. We could hear music coming from the TV as the DVD started up and, as we approached, the title and opening credits were on the screen with a portion of the screen showing a video sample, presumably giving a taste of what was to come or, more aptly, "cum". It showed a close-up of and engorged knob spurting white semen in a strong jet. It was only a second or two long, but played over and over, making it look like the knob's owner was having an endless orgasm.

"It looks good so far," Russell said, with a tone of voice probably covering a little embarrassment. He, a bit like me, was dithering about where to sit. The layout of our TV area is that it caters pretty much just for the two of us. There's a large sofa directly facing the screen, and fairly close. The sofa has big solid upholstered arms at each end that can double as a place to sit if you have to. There are other chairs nearby, but not arranged as TV viewing spots. Those details all contributed to how the seating arrangements amongst the four of us were arranged.

"You boys put your towels on the sofa and sit down," Jan instructed. "You're the main audience, after all." I handed over Jan's towel to her as she settled herself on one end, gesturing to Eva and saying, "You pop yourself down that other end, and I'll run the buttons from here." As Russell and I still dithered a bit, Jan said, "Come on, come on, sit down you two. The show's starting." With that, she pressed the play button. Both Russell and I looked a bit embarrassed yet were captured by the situation. And, I think it also fair to say that I was interested in where this might be going and, probably, Russell was too.

We settled onto the sofa, me at Jan's end and Russell at Eva's end. The video took no time to get right into the topic material. The first scene was a close-up of a hard cock across the full screen with the knob red and engorged. I presume the guy was lying down. A woman's thumb could be seen just under the upper edge of the knob and her finger tips just resting on that exquisitely sensitive daggy bit of skin just below the knob on the underside. She was very gentle. No mad pumping or tugging, just a light stroking of her fingers a centimeter or two back and forth. The guy must have been close because he came in a few seconds. Huge gobs of white jizz spurted, about eight or nine pulses in all, during which the woman made no sound but the guy did, starting with a guttural "uuhh" just before the first spurt as he must have felt himself going over the edge, and then a quieter but unmistakable "uh, uh, uh" noises synchronised with his orgasmic pulsing.

I must say I enjoyed the scene. Maybe it sounds kinky, and I'm not bisexual, but I have always liked seeing an aroused cock come. I think it must be to do with the empathy a guy always feels when thinking about what the cock's owner must be feeling. There's no feeling like it in the world. Jan likes her share of porn, too, though it's not a large part of her erotic agenda and, when she watches, I know that she likes the male cum-shots, too.

That first scene must have only taken 15 seconds or so. It was followed immediately by another. And another. As this was happening there was some repartee amongst the four of us, I think at that stage partly to cover some embarrassment that we were watching this at all. "I bet he enjoyed that," Jan said. Eva agreed, glancing at Russell and adding, "Sure looked like it. What do you think, Baby? Worth the money so far?"

"It certainly has intellectual and artistic promise," Russell answered in his fake academic voice, and we found ourselves looking at the next scene, and the next.

It really was a great hand-job video. There was lots of variety in hand action, body position and so on. Something I liked was that many of the shots were close-up, and many were gently coaxing of the cum from the engorged, aroused cock, not frenzied jerking. I found it quite arousing, and also found that I couldn't exactly hide the fact.

All men know that you can suppress sexual arousal for a while, depending on circumstances. Mostly we don't get inappropriate erections at the beach, for example (even at nude beaches) or when we are obliged to get naked under more clinical circumstances. Since your brain is your largest erogenous zone, mostly it keeps arousal at bay when it has to. But, it succumbs to arousal eventually if the stimulus is right, even if the circumstances are wrong. I was in exactly that situation. I was enjoying the video, seeing the hard cocks spurt. Remember, I was there in the nude with my wife and another couple, also in the nude. We'd had a day of sexual innuendo and repartee, and I guess my hormones were just ready for something rather than nothing. I felt that twinge all men will know well, when that little valve (or whatever it is) in your limp penis opens, just a bit at first, and blood starts to swell in. It doesn't need to be much. But you know it when you feel it. I felt it. I ignored it for a few seconds, thought of England and prime numbers, but I was losing the battle. I suppose if I had deliberately made some excuse, got up and ended my video watching, I could have extricated myself at that point, but for whatever reason, I didn't. I went on watching those spurts of cum. And went on slightly expanding in my groin. I could feel the little pulses going in.

I only had a semi at that stage, but it was enough to embarrass me. I was sitting next to Russell, as I said, but didn't want to explicitly turn to look at his crotch to see how he was faring. So, rather pathetically, I just ended up covering myself with my hands. It don't recall exactly what I said, but it was something like, "It's working a bit too well on me, I'm afraid. Russell was right. I am beginning to embarrass myself."

"Goodness, you're blushing," Jan blurted, unhelpfully, as she looked directly at my face. "Don't worry about it. It's good to know the thing is worth the money." She looked over to Eva, and added, "How's your man going over there?"

Russell answered himself, saying "About to share the same problem, I fear," moving to cover his own penis which, as I glanced, didn't seem even to be a semi. As I said earlier, Russell has a sort of hidden penis so any state of semi-ness he had was invisible at that moment. Maybe he really felt it, or was just reacting in sympathy with my plight.

"Well, I think it's silly of both of them, don't you?" Jan directed to Eva. "Speaking for myself, I rather like the idea of seeing how well the video works. I won't be embarrassed."

"Neither will I," Eva responded from the other end of the couch, "So take your hands away and stop being babies." With that she playfully reached down and swatted Russell's hands away from his crotch. With a rueful "what the heck?" smile, Russell's hands moved to his sides as Jan said to me,"You too, Mister. Behind your back. Let's enjoy the show." She grinned hugely, first at me, then at Eva.

That final remark about "enjoying the show" was dripping with ambiguity. I must be slow on the uptake because it actually took me a few seconds to process that "more" had just arrived in our lounge room. It may seem odd if you haven't done it, but being in nude company is not, of itself, all that sexy or erotic. Sure, you can enjoy looking at the body parts, and I had been enjoying seeing Eva's jutting nipples throughout the lunch, much I presume as Russell had been enjoying Jan's shapely bottom, nice boobs and hairless pubes. But that's not the same as "sexy" or "erotic". What finally struck me after my few seconds of mental processing was that the four of us had crossed a line and were now in the territory of "sexy and erotic".

Jan and I had wanted nude friends with "more", and here it was. Now the nudity mattered in a new way. I was sitting beside my lovely naked wife, her breasts at my eye level only inches away. Eva, likewise, was perched nakedly on the other end of the couch, her smile taking in Russell and me. And, best of all, we two guys were naked between them and being given permission, in fact being encouraged, to get erections while our wives took in the view. This was definitely the land of "more". Erections more often than not lead to a happy ending, and I was now in the zone of anticipating that. If Russell and I continued to "enjoy" the video, our display of manhood would be the live part of the show, one way or another.

Whilst this thinking had been going on in my head, the video had continued to play. There was scene after scene of stroking and ejaculating. Silence amongst us settled for a couple of minutes as we all continued to watch the screen. I wasn't any more than slightly semi when we had that discussion, and had wilted a bit in the meantime, but the situation had changed profoundly. My wife wanted me to "enjoy" the show and, so it seemed, Eva wanted that, too, for Russell. So, the inevitable began to happen. I started to fill up, slowly but inexorably, and now wanting it to happen. Once it starts, as guys know, it feels nice and is self-fulfilling (pardon the pun). The harder you get, the nicer it feels to get that bit harder still. And I wanted a hard-on that did me proud.

As I watched some on-screen fingers coax a multi-spurt orgasm out of yet another anonymous cock, I found myself saying, "Well, the video's working well on me," as my cock swelled to semi, then past that, to be hard and erect, my knob full and throbbing. Because of the way I was sitting, my knob was pointing to my belly button, touching my stomach but hard enough to rise a little away on its own as my heart beat. "That's very good, dear," Jan said. "I'm sure Eva approves."

"Russell is enjoying it too, it seems," Eva reported from her end of the sofa. Russell didn't say anything. I didn't want to be too obvious but stole a glance at my guest sharing this bizarre situation with me or, more correctly, stole a glance at his crotch. His earlier almost-invisible penis was now quite visible, not very long but thick at the root, poking out from a frizz of red pubic hair. Unlike me, where my knob is on full view all the time, Russell is uncircumcised but his erection was enthusiastic enough for his knob to be bulbous, purple and unmistakably on display. Like me, he was oozing pre-cum.

Sure, it was exciting and erotic, but it was also agony. I was so engorged that I was on a hair trigger. Guys will know the feeling of that little inner twitch that could send you over the edge at any moment, and these were starting to happen. I felt that I would come no-hands if so much as a breath of air passed too near my cock. I desperately wanted some relief from the excruciatingly wonderful throbbing sensation that was now consuming my every thought. I knew I couldn't go on with this game much longer.

"God, this is agony," I moaned, looking up at Jan. I must have had a convincingly pathetic look on my face because she said, in a baby, cooing-style voice, "Does somebody want something?" She paused. "Perhaps Willy wants some attention like on the TV?" I could barely speak, and didn't know what to say. The answer, of course, was yes, yes, YES but it was still, despite the situation, a little awkward and embarrassing in front of our guests to say so. But the truth was I wanted to come, desperately needed to come, and very much liked the idea of doing so with Eva watching. I guess that was the exhibitionist aspect to it, and I was oh-so-ready.

"Perhaps I should put him out of his misery," Jan said, looking towards Eva, and then, to me, said, "Would you like me to show you what I've learned from this very excellent video, darling?"

Pushing my head back into the sofa and looking up at the ceiling I moaned, "Yes. Yes. I can't stand this." With that, my lovely, sexy, naked wife sitting on the edge of the sofa reached out her right hand.

"Now, let's see if I have the idea," she said. I watched, mesmerised, as the tip of her extended middle finger descended and touched the blob of pre-cum glistening on the very tip of my engorged knob. She did this oh-so-lightly, but it felt electric. "You certainly look ready. I mightn't need to do much at all," she teased.

Using only the now-wet fingertip, she moved her touch away from the urethra opening and trailed it down towards the underside of my cock. As any guy knows, there is that magic, sensitive spot just below where the knob ends on that daggy bit of skin on the underside which is the centre-point of the greatest pleasure in the world. Jan's fingertip made that journey, gently and very slowly, probably taking about three or four seconds to cover the distance of maybe an inch. When her finger arrived there, and stopped, I was ready to explode or have a heart attack.

"If I rub a little bit, just here, I think that might work." Jan was speaking softly, almost cooing these words. "We've seen the video. Now you can show us what you have stored up in there." As she spoke, with very gentle pressure, she began softly circling her fingertip on that magic spot. Nothing else. No jerks. No squeezes. Just that gentle touch, slowly around, and around, and.....

I am embarrassed to say I had no staying power at all. After, literally, a scant few seconds of her fingertip rub I knew I was going to shoot. Guys know the feeling. Your penis feels throbbingly full, with the centre of pleasure just where Jan's fingertip was doing its thing. Then, it starts deep down in the root of your penis; that almost-pain that gathers and tightens, a sensation like pulling-in as the muscles in your groin gather, and then the pressure builds, and builds, and you know you are powerless over it. In a strong orgasm the building thunderhead of pressure boarders on pain as it reaches its peak. It's a strange mixture of almost wanting it to stop, but also not wanting it to, wanting instead for it to grow just that bit more intense before you tip over into the contractions. There's no feeling in the world like it.

Waves of powerful, pulsing pleasure force their way up the length of your engorged cock, carrying a load of hot semen with them, culminating in that excruciating ultimate pulse of pleasure on the underside of the knob, right where Jan was rubbing me. I lost track of what Jan or others may have said at this point, or whether or not I was making any noise. (Jan told me later I grunted in an 'ughh', 'ughh' sort of way as I came.) The centre of my attention was in my penis which pulsed deliciously as a huge spurt of semen erupted from my knob, followed by another and another as Jan's fingertip continued its little circular rubbing motion. At my age I don't have in me the eight or ten spurts common in porn films, with three being more my average these days. But that day, I know I spurted at least five good wads of hot semen because I saw them as well as felt them. After a few seconds, the delicious pulses subsided.

Jan knows how unbearable it is for a man to be stimulated when they've just come, and stopped her circling motions at the right time. My leg and stomach muscles which had been tensed then relaxed as I sank back deeper into the sofa in a post-orgasmic stupor.

"It looks like you enjoyed that," Jan said in perfect understatement as she used the corner of my towel to wipe away most of the pool of white goo that had gathered on my stomach and which was now starting to ooze down my side. "Nearly as good as the movies, I'd say."

"At least as good," Eva added from her end of the sofa. "And I know somebody who needs to finish the show for us."

I hadn't really been taking much notice of Russell for the last couple of minutes, as you will understand. Now that I was coming down from my orgasmic build-up, with the extreme eroticism of what had brought us to this point ebbing away, at least for me, I noticed he was sitting much as before, not saying anything, with his short, thick dick on full view and no doubt in the same or worse condition as I had been. And he'd had the added 'benefit' of seeing Jan bring me off which, given his taste in DVDs, was likely to have added to his state of arousal.

Eva reached out her left hand and gently encircled the thick root of Russell's penis. "You've been a very good boy all day, so I think a reward is coming," she said.

Jan and I were openly watching as Eva, leaning forward, tightened her grip and slowly masturbated Russell's cock. Russell gave a sort of grunting moan and looked straight ahead as his wife's hand rhythmically caressed him. Her style was interesting. She pulled down hard on his shaft, the motion almost a jerk, then held the pressure there in a pause at the end of the downward motion which saw the foreskin very tight and the knob fully exposed, its sensitive underside stretched tight. Then, she released the pressure and gave him a very slow upstroke, her hand sliding right up the tip, pulling some foreskin with it to cover and enclose the knob. A pause, and couple of sudden squeezes at this point, and the process began again with the hard down-stroke.

As she proceeded with her ministrations, Eva continued talking. "Your DVD has been great entertainment. It's your turn now. Show us all what you can do, Big Boy."

Russell lasted longer than I did, but still not too long. I'd guess about one minute. With long experience with her partner, probably Eva could tell Russell was ready to blow before we did, but Jan and I picked up on the verbal moan, a deep throaty sound that could only mean one thing. We saw his eyes shut, head go back and muscles tense as he pushed his groin forward and up, lifting slightly from the sofa. Eva suddenly changed pace then, giving him a series of very fast up-and-down strokes as white jizz erupted from his penis in large messy globs that went this way and that, spattering Russell's pubic hair, his stomach and Eva's hand. His orgasm went on for several seconds, and then Eva's hand stopped its motion as Russell fell back with a relaxed grunt, much as I had done a few minutes before.

"Clever boy. Well done," Eva said to Russell as she used a loose bit of his towel to wipe her hands and clean him up.

"Good show all round, fellas," Jan added. "Now, I guess you're both exhausted and could do with a drink. I know I could." With that she clicked off the DVD which was still rolling its ejaculations but which none of us had taken any notice of for several minutes. "You guys get yourselves tidy while I get us a refill." She headed off into the kitchen. Eva announced she was off to the bathroom for a moment as Russell and I got up and looked a bit sheepishly at each other, not being quite sure what to say. We made our way back to the patio table without really saying anything, but with some dabbing at our respective damp spots and wiping down as we went.

* * *

You might think that with an orgasmic ice-breaker as we'd just experienced, the rest of the day would have automatically turned into an exciting orgy of sexual excess, but it was nothing like that. Instead, if you'll pardon the pun, it was a bit of an anti-climax. Perhaps it sounds odd, but when we regrouped on the patio we didn't actually discuss what had just happened. Looking back, I think we were probably all a little surprised and embarrassed at the turn of events. We chatted about nothing in particular and before long the day was drawing to a close and it was time for us to get dressed and see our friends off. There was a moment of double entendre levity as Russell, getting into his car, said, "Lovely day, guys. Sorry to come and go." With that, we all pecked on cheeks and shook hands respectively, and they were gone.

A couple of weeks went by and we were invited back to their place for lunch. It was a lovely day. There was no ambiguity any longer about whether we would go nude at these social encounters and we simply "nuded up" (as we nudists day) shortly after arrival. Soon we found ourselves once again enjoying their poolside entertainment area with drinks and nibbles, with lunch on the agenda shortly.

This time, the chat was more personal than it had been on our previous meetings. It was Eva who led the way, saying how much they had both enjoyed the time at our house and how pleased she was to have found some friends with whom they could have some adult fun.

"We thought your web profile was close to ours," she said, "and hoped that what you were looking for was the same as we wanted to find." She finished, "I think it's called friends with benefits," and looked a bit embarrassed as she smiled at both Jan and me.

I can't recall the exact conversation, and it doesn't matter really. Over the next few minutes we all chimed in to a discussion about the nudist website, what people say in their profiles, and what they actually mean as they say it. We ranged a bit more widely than just that, too, by sipping our wine and philosophising a little about what older adults like ourselves want in relationships. It turns out we were very similar; monogamously attached to our spouses but excited by the idea of some fresh eroticism with likeminded, friendly people in ways that are fun, sexy and harm no-one. With that, we drank a joint toast to how clever we'd been to stumble across one another.

That discussion didn't lay out explicitly any ground rules about what was "in" and "out" of bounds. That was all left unstated and fuzzy. We certainly weren't agreeing to all become swingers and swap partners for an orgy after lunch. But we were giving ourselves permission to be sexy in each other's company, to excite ourselves and share that excitement for the pleasure of the others, and to explore some of our fantasies. Basically, we all wanted to enjoy being naughty again before we grew too old to remember how.

Russell was to be the cook for our BBQ lunch. "Let's have a dip in the pool before I cover this overweight body with an apron and turn into a chef," he suggested. With the day warm and the pool inviting, the idea was readily accepted.

As Jan and I bobbed about in the water, we remarked to each other how well this had turned out, and how fortunate we'd been to find these nice people with whom we seemed to click so well. As Jan and I lazed back and forth, Russell and Eva were further towards the shallow end, cuddling each other. We soon noticed that our hosts' cuddle was altering into something else. We both looked at each other, then back at them. Even though we couldn't see their lower bodies, there was no doubt what was going on at the shallow end of the pool. They were having sex. Eva had her back to Russell as she held on to the edge of the pool, as he held her by the sides of her bottom and rhythmically moved his hips to and fro, sloshing waves back and forth as he did so.

"Should we watch or give them some privacy?" Jan asked me quietly, as we trod water at our end.

"Watch, of course," was my reply. "That's what they want us to do." I added, "And then they'll want to watch us."

"Sounds fine to me," my lovely wife said. So we moved closer, and watched.

* End *

Here is a sample from another story you may enjoy:

MORE THAN
She Can Take

EROTICA SHORT STORIES, VOL.28

JUST PLAIN BOB

I never did tell Lois that she had been busted. I just accepted the fact that she was an unfaithful whore and let it go. I had no idea how long it had been going on and no idea why. I had thought that we had a good marriage and I know, or at least I thought I did, that there was nothing wrong with our sex life. We made love three and sometimes four times a week, sometimes twice in a night and I was willing to do anything that she wanted. What was important, however, is that the marriage was dead – not over, just dead.

Why not over? Because I didn't have the energy for it. I'd been married once before and my first divorce had ruined me financially and had made me into an emotional basket case for years. If I was thirty-five or forty, I might have done it, but not at fifty. Why start over? Lois kept a clean house, was a good cook, and did the laundry and all the other things that a wife does to make life move smoothly. We didn't argue or fight so I just decided to settle for a comfortable existence. So I said nothing about what I saw and life went on.

The only change was that I stopped having sex with Lois. When she asked why, I told her that I was having some problems and was seeing a doctor. After two months, I told her that I had acute erectile dysfunction and that I couldn't get a hard on. Another two months went by and then I told her that I had tried everything that the doctor had suggested, but that nothing worked and she would just have to get used to the fact that the sexual part of our marriage was over. She wasn't really happy about it, but I really didn't give a shit about how she felt about it.

I didn't give up sex though. There was a woman I went to high school with and she had lost her husband in the First Gulf War and she supplemented her income by servicing a few select customers and I paid her a visit twice a week.

***

Lois and I were in the habit of going out for breakfast every

Saturday and Sunday and we always ate at the same restaurant. The place was just around the corner from where I worked and I had lunch in there two or three times during the week. There was a waitress working there named Tiffany and she was a lot of fun to be around. A tall girl, almost six feet, and with a hard, tight body to die for. She had the goods and she knew how to dress to show them off. Low hip-huggers and tops that emphasized her high breasts and flat stomach. She had a wild side to her and she had several tattoos and a piercing or two that she also loved to show off.

I got in the habit of flirting with her at lunchtime and after a couple of months, we had developed a rapport. The flirting progressed from the simple to the borderline raunchy and Tiff gave as good as she got. She had a stud through her tongue and one day I said, "One of these days you are going to have to explain or better yet, show me what the purpose of that thing is."

She stuck her tongue out at me and said, "First you will have to show me that your health insurance is up to date. When I put you in the hospital I want to know that you'll be taken care of."

One day when I came in after not stopping in for a week, she came up to my table and lifted her top to show me that she'd had her navel pierced and was sporting what looked like a diamond stick pin.

"You know, Tiff, I have a barely controllable urge to kiss your belly."

If you enjoyed this sample then look for More Than She Can Take.

Also by this Author:

<u>Fun in the Park</u>
<u>Naughty Mojo</u>

About the Author

Leon and his wife met at grade school and were friends throughout that period. When grown, their lives went in different directions. Recently, in middle age, they reconnected and were married after a divorce for Leon and many years of widowhood for his wife.

They are very much in love, with a great sex life which includes an interest in safe, fun ways to involve other individuals and couples around their age. Leon is the writer but the stories are theirs, mixing real situations and some fictional embellishments to provide entertaining and stimulating reading whilst also giving confidence to middle-aged couples and individuals that have erotic experiences shared with other consenting adults are normal, fun, safe and possible.

Check my page on Amazon and my blog for Updates and interesting info.

Author Central - http://www.amazon.com/Leon-Randall/e/B00A49YAY4/ref=ntt_athr_dp_pel_pop_1
Author Blog - http://leon-randall.awesomeauthors.org/

If you enjoyed any of my books then please share the love and click like on my books in Amazon.

If you write me a review and send me an email I will send you a free book, or many.
(Just know that these emails are filtered by my publisher.)

Good news is always welcome.

One Last Thing, For Kindle Readers...

When you turn the page, Kindle will give you the opportunity to rate this book and share your thoughts on Facebook and Twitter. If you enjoyed my writings, would you please take a few seconds to let your friends know about it? Because... when they enjoy they will be grateful to you and so will I.

Thank You!

Leon Randall
leon_randall@awesomeauthors.org

www.ingramcontent.com/pod-product-compliance
Lightning Source LLC
Chambersburg PA
CBHW071353130626
46556CB00005B/2170